Enid Blyton's
A Christmas Wish

ILLUSTRATED BY MAGGIE DOWNER

A TEMPLAR BOOK

Produced by The Templar Company plc, Pippbrook Mill, London Road, Dorking, Surrey RH4 1JE

Text copyright © *A Christmas Wish* 1926-1953 by Darrell Waters Limited
This edition illustration and design copyright © 1995 by The Templar Company plc
Enid Blyton's signature mark is a registered trademark of Darrell Waters Limited

This edition produced for Parragon Book Service Ltd, Unit 13-17, Avonbridge Trading Estate, Atlantic Road, Avonmouth, Bristol BS11 9QD

This book contains material first published as *The Lost Wishing Cap* in Enid Blyton's Sunny Stories
and Sunny Stories between 1926 and 1953.

Printed and bound in Great Britain

ISBN 0-75251-068-1

Once upon a time there was a poor boy named Sam. He lived in the far North in a little house made entirely of wood. He had four little sisters and four little brothers, all younger than he was. His father had died several years before, and Sam and his mother had to work very hard to get food for them all to eat.

They had worked hard all year and now it was nearly Christmas time. All the children were getting very excited. One day, they stopped to gaze at a brightly lit shop window.

"Look at the beautiful decorations!" cried Sam's youngest sister.

"Look at all the delicious food!" cried his twin brothers together.

"And, oh, *look* at all the lovely toys!" cried a third. "Sam, shall we have toys and good things to eat this Christmas?"

"I don't know," said Sam. "They cost a lot of money, and it is as much as we can do to buy bread. But if I can buy you toys, then you know that I will."

Sam didn't really think he would be able to buy his brothers and sisters what they wanted, even though it was his own heart's desire. His mother had been ill for many weeks and could not work, so they had not been able to save any money for Christmas presents. Sam doubted that they would even have enough to buy some special food for Christmas Day – a turkey, perhaps, or a plump plum pudding.

But he was a cheerful
little boy and didn't
give up hope, so
out he went to
work every
day with
a smile.

As he was walking along, Sam planned what he would do if only he could save some money from his wages.

"I'd buy a beautiful scarf and some chocolates for mother, and a toy each for the boys and girls," he thought.

"And I'd buy some lovely food for all of us. How nice that would be!"

But Christmas came nearer and nearer, and still Sam had no money to buy anything. Try as he might, he couldn't seem to save even a penny and as the days ticked by he began to look worried.

At last Christmas Eve came, and Sam knew his little brothers and sisters would have to go without toys or turkey. He was very sad as he walked slowly home after his long day's work.

It was late and very dark, and the snow lay thick on the ground. Huge, feathery snowflakes fell softly against his cheeks, and he wrapped his coat more tightly round him, for it was cold.

He shivered as the snow seeped through his worn-out boots, making his feet feel like lumps of ice. Poor Sam! This was surely the most dismal Christmas he had ever known.

Suddenly there came a sound of sleigh-bells, and down the road glided a sleigh drawn by reindeer. It went past so quickly that Sam couldn't see who was driving it. But as the sleigh passed him, something dropped at his feet, blown there by the wind.

Sam picked it up and looked
at it by the light of his lamp.
It was made of soft red velvet,
trimmed with white fur.
"It's a cap!" cried Sam.
"The driver of that sleigh
must have lost it in the
wind. I'll see if he comes
back for it."

But though Sam waited a long time, no one came, so at last he went home with the red cap in his pocket.

He was wet through with the snow, and his feet were frozen solid with the cold as he wiped his boots on the mat at home.

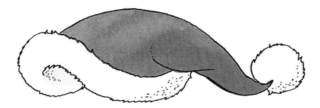

His youngest sister, Sarah, who had been tucked up in bed, ran to greet him with a hug and a kiss. The rest of the children were fast asleep.

"You must be freezing, Sam," said his mother when she saw him. "And look at your poor wet feet!"

"Yes," said Sam, sighing. "My boots are nearly worn out now. I wish I had a new pair!"

And whatever do you think! Just as he said that, his old boots flew out of the door, and a pair of brand-new ones flew in!

Sam stared in disbelief. His mother rubbed her eyes, and looked again and again – but it was true. There stood a pair of fine new boots.

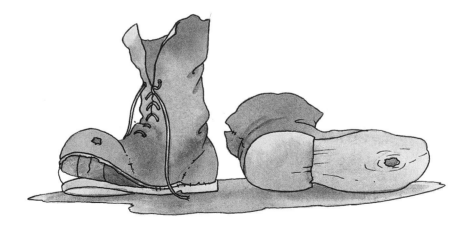

"This is magic," said Sam. "But I wish *you* could have a pair of fine new boots as well, mother dear!"

And almost before he had finished speaking, in flew another pair of boots which landed right next to the first! The two stared at them in amazement.

"Well, well!" said Sam's mother. "This is certainly magic. But where is it coming from! Have you been speaking to pixies, my boy?"

"Oh no, mother," said Sam. Then he suddenly remembered the red cap in his pocket, and he pulled it out.

"Maybe it has something to do with this," he said, and told his mother how he had found it. "It must be a wishing cap!" said Sam joyfully. "Oh, mother! We'll wish for toys and a turkey, shall we? And oh! I *would* like a nice warm fire to dry myself by!"

Immediately a great fire blazed up in the chimney, and Sam hurried over to it, laughing happily.

But his mother looked worried and took the soft velvet cap from his hands.

"Sam," she said. "This is someone else's wishing cap, not ours. The owner of it may be looking everywhere for it. We must give it back at once and not use it to wish for more things for ourselves."

"But how do we find who it belongs to, mother?" asked Sam.

"Well, you've only got to wish that the owner was here, and the wishing cap will bring him," she replied, handing the cap back to her son.

Sam knew she was right. It would be wrong to keep a wishing cap belonging to someone else. So he wished once again.

"I wish the owner of this cap was here," he said loudly.

And can you guess who seconds later was standing there in front of them. Why, there in the middle of the floor, stood Santa Claus himself! Sam and his mother could hardly believe their eyes.

Santa looked very surprised at first, but when he saw his red cap in Sam's hands, he understood what had happened.

"So *you* found my hat!" he said, smiling. And he broke into such a loud and jolly laugh that it brought all the younger children running from their beds. How surprised they were to find Santa standing there.

"This is a piece of luck!' smiled Santa. "For I need my cap especially tonight. You see, when my sack of toys gets empty, I wish it full again!"

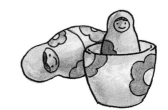

Sam stared at Santa Claus in delight. Fancy the wishing cap belonging to *him*! He gave it back with a smile.

"I'm sorry to say we got two pairs of boots and this warm fire by using your cap," said Sam. "I hope it hasn't done the magic in it any harm."

"Bless you, no!" laughed Santa. "It was splendid of you to wish to find the owner.

Lots of people wouldn't have done that. But if you'd kept my cap for yourself, you'd soon have found that it brought you bad luck and unhappiness, instead of good fortune and joy. Thank you very much for giving it back to me. Now I must be off. I have a hundred thousand homes to visit tonight!"

Off went the jolly man, tramping out into the snow, and then Sam heard the sound of sleigh bells going down the road.

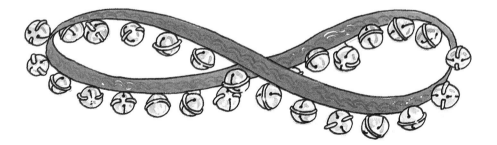

Next morning you should have heard the shrieks and shouts and squeaks and squeals of joy in Sam's home! Everybody's stocking was full to the brim with the things they wanted most – and Sam had a huge pile of presents on his bed too.

His mother found a lovely red scarf and a purse full of money in her stocking – and when she went downstairs she gasped in surprise. On the table lay the biggest turkey she had ever seen, a monster plum-pudding and plates full of mince pies! "Thank you, Santa!" she whispered.

All round them were apples and oranges, sweets and chocolate, and in the far corner was a Christmas tree, hung with more presents. And who do you think was on the top of the tree?

Why, a little Santa Claus
dressed in red, smiling
at all the happy
children.

"*Wasn't* it a good thing I found that wishing cap!" said Sam.

"And wasn't it a good thing you found the owner!" said his mother.

"Yes!" chorused the children, dancing up and down in excitement. "Now we're going to have the best Christmas Day ever. Aren't we the luckiest family in the whole world?"

They all had a perfectly lovely Christmas after that, and when they were dancing round the tree in the evening, they suddenly heard a chuckling laugh. It sounded just like Santa Claus!

But he wasn't anywhere in the room, and
Sam thought it *must* have been the little
Santa Claus stuck on the top of the tree.
  I wonder if it was, don't you?